MW01100976

© Aladdin Books Ltd 2001

Designed and produced by
Aladdin Books Ltd
28 Percy Street
London W1P 0LD

First published in
the United States in 2001 by
Copper Beech Books,
an imprint of
The Millbrook Press
2 Old New Milford Road
Brookfield, Connecticut 06804

ISBN 0-7613-2173-X

Cataloging-in-Publication data is on
file at the Library of Congress

Printed in Belgium
All rights reserved

Coordinator
Jim Pipe

Design
Flick, Book Design and Graphics

Picture Research
Brian Hunter Smart

My World

Games I Play

by Tammy J. Schlepp

Copper Beech Books
Brookfield, Connecticut

toys
and
games

2

Today my friend Jerry is coming over to play.

We like to run and play in the yard. But today it is raining.

What shall we play?

toy box

"Let's play dress-up," I say.

"I will be a beautiful princess."

"OK," says Jerry.

"I want to be a knight!"

dress-up clothes

Mom's old gown is too big for me.
But I feel like a princess.

Mom finds Jerry a helmet. "You
might meet a dragon!" she says.

dressing
up

"What shall we play?" says Jerry.

"Let's build a castle," I say.

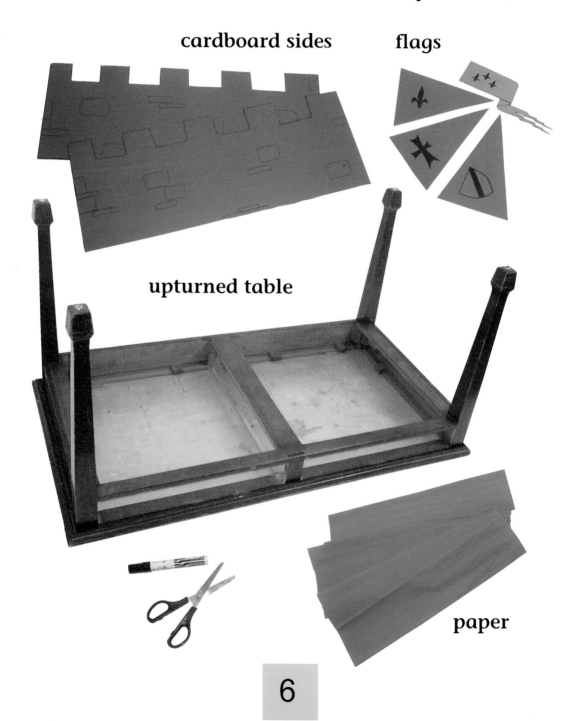

cardboard sides

flags

upturned table

paper

Mom helps us put the
castle together.

"Now we are safe
from dragons," says Jerry.

castle

We leave our castle and peek outside. The sun is out!

"Come on, Liz. Let's jump on the trampoline," says Jerry.

on the trampoline

Next we play hopscotch.

I throw a stone. I hop, hop, hop all the way to the end.

I stand on one leg and pick up the stone.

hopscotch

"Your brother is playing soccer.
Do you want to watch?" Dad asks.

"Can we play too?" I ask. "You
can play after the game," says Dad.

soccer game

At the game, I cheer for Will's team. "Go, Will!" I shout.

The players take a rest at halftime. Jerry and I play catch with the ball.

playing catch

After the game, Will plays with us.

He kicks the ball to me.

Then I kick the ball to Jerry.

"Shoot!" says Will. Jerry kicks the ball hard. It goes into the net!

"It's a goal!" I shout.

scoring a goal

in the car

Dad drives us home in the car.

"What shall we play?" I ask.

"Let's play I Spy," says Dad.

"Will, you go first."

"I spy with my little eye, something beginning with W," says Will.

We all look out the car window. What begins with a W?

looking out of the car

"Tree," says Dad.

We laugh.
"Tree doesn't
begin with a W,"
says Will.

tree

window

"Window,"
says Jerry.

"Yes,"
says Will.
"You got it!"

16

"Now it's Jerry's turn to ask,"
says Dad.

"I spy something that begins with B,"
says Jerry. Can you see what it is?

At home, Mom is cooking dinner.
"What shall we play now?" I ask.

"How about a game of
checkers?" says Dad.

playing
checkers

I move the black pieces and Jerry moves the white.

Can you see where I can jump over Jerry's piece?

checkerboard

It is time for dinner, and Jerry goes home.

After dinner, we play Go Fish. Mom helps me sort my cards.

playing cards

After our game, I start to yawn.

"It's time for a sleepy girl and her teddy to go to bed," says Dad. "You can play again tomorrow."

teddy

Here are some words and phrases from the book.

castle

dress up

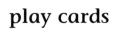

play cards

look in the toy box

jump on the
trampoline

hopscotch

kick the ball

play checkers

Can you use these words to
write your own story?

Did you see these in the book?

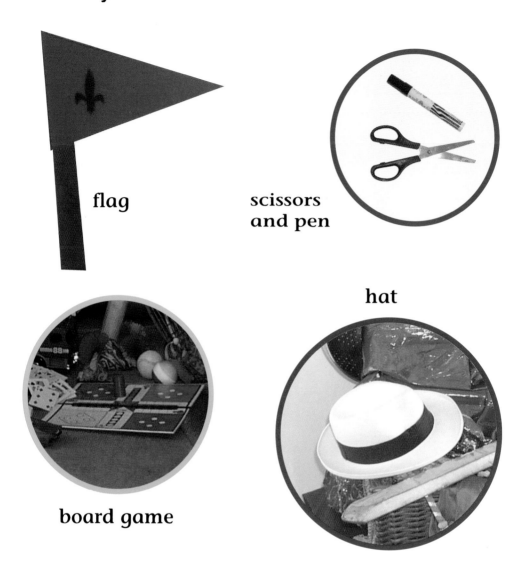

flag

scissors
and pen

hat

board game

Illustrator: Mary Lonsdale for SGA

Picture Credits:
Abbreviations: t–top, m–middle, b–bottom, r–right, l–left, c–center.
2, 4, 6-7, 10, 15, 16 both, 17, 19, 21, 22, 24 all–Select Pictures.
8, 23tl–Corbis.